SURPRISE, ANGELICA!

Based on the TV series *Rugrats®* created by Arlene Klasky, Gabor Csupo, and Paul Germain as seen on Nickelodeon®

ISBN 0-439-17363-9

12 11 10 9 8 7 6 5 4 3 2 1   0 1 2 3 4 5/0

Printed in the U.S.A.

First Scholastic printing, April 2000

SURPRISE, ANGELICA!

by Becky Gold
illustrated by Vince Giarrano

SCHOLASTIC INC.

New York   Toronto   London   Auckland   Sydney
Mexico City   New Delhi   Hong Kong

"Get it, Spike!" Tommy called to his dog. He threw a ball in the air. Spike caught it. "Good boy!"

"Catching a ball is nothing," said Angelica. "Susie's new gerbils play *inside* balls."

"What are germ balls?" Tommy asked.

"Not germ balls, *gerbils*," Angelica replied. "They're a kind of rat who live in dark caves. And Susie has invited me over to see them."

"That sounds scary, Angelica!" exclaimed Chuckie.

Just then Tommy's mom, Didi, called
them in. "Susie's here," she said.

"Can we see Susie's gerbils, too?"
Tommy asked Angelica.

"You babies stay here," Angelica warned.
"Gerbils are very dangerous. They have
sharp teeth that can chew through
anything—high chairs . . . 'frigegators . . .
everything!"

"Everything?" Chuckie gasped.

"That's right, Finster," Angelica said.

She wanted to be the first to see the gerbils.

"Hey, you two are shivering like Jell-O," Susie said when she saw the babies. "What's the matter?"

"Susie, aren't you afraid to live with cave rats?" Chuckie asked.

"Yeah," said Tommy, 'specially ones with shark teeth?"

"You mean the gerbils? Why don't you come over to meet them?"

Tommy and Chuckie shook their heads. Susie stared at Angelica. She had a feeling she knew why they weren't coming over.

"So, Susie," said Angelica, "ready to go?"

"Tell you what," Susie said, "I'll go home first and prepare the gerbils for your visit. They don't like surprises. I'll come get you when they're ready."

"Oh, okay," Angelica said.

"Why she gots to repair them, Angelica?" asked Tommy.

"Yeah," Phil said. "Maybe they're broke."

"Maybe they gots too many germs!" Chuckie exclaimed.

"She said *prepare*, not repair, you dumb babies!" said Angelica.

When Susie got home, she told her brother Edwin how Angelica had scared Tommy, Chuckie, Phil, and Lil.

"Well, Suse," Edwin replied, "maybe Angelica just needs a taste of her own medicine. Come on, I'll help you."

After a while, Angelica started getting antsy. Those gerbils must be prepared enough, she thought. She went next door and rang the bell. Susie answered.

"I was just coming to get you," said Susie, huffing and puffing.

"Why are you breathing funny?" Angelica asked.

"I was running to get the gerbils more things to chew," Susie explained, "They're teething like crazy!"

"What's that?" asked Angelica. She pointed to the floor. It was covered with big, gray spots.

"Gerbil tracks," Susie said.

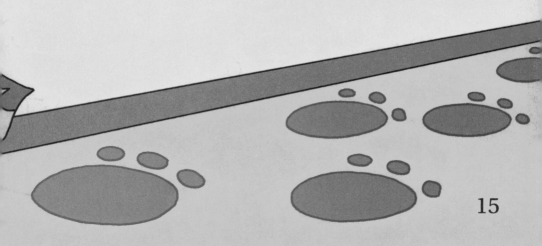

"Uh . . . is that their food?" asked
Angelica.

"Just a snack for later," Susie replied.
"This is Frankenrat's bowl . . . and this is
Igor's," she said, pointing. "And these are
boxes for them to chew on."

"Susie," said Angelica, "maybe the gerbils need to chew some more. Maybe they aren't ready to meet me yet. Maybe . . . we should go play outside!"

"No," Susie said. "They've been waiting for you! Follow me!" She led Angelica upstairs.

Suddenly they heard a loud growl,
followed by angry snarls. Angelica didn't
know that Edwin was behind the door
making the noises. She ran back down
the stairs.

The doorbell rang again. It was Tommy, Chuckie, Phil, and Lil.

"Hi, gang!" Susie said.

"We were afraid," Tommy told her, "but a baby gots to be brave."

"So you're all ready to meet the gerbils?" Susie asked.

"YEAH!" cried Tommy, Phil, and Lil.

"N-n-no," said Chuckie.

"Hey, where's Angelica?" Tommy wondered.

"I don't know," said Susie. "She was here a minute ago."

"Who made the big poker dots?" asked Phil.

"Edwin did," Susie answered. "Come on upstairs."

"Oh, no," Chuckie mumbled. "I don't want to go up there!"

"Ooooooh!" exclaimed Lil.

"They don't look like rats," said Phil.

"And this doesn't look like a cave," added Lil.

"Gerbils aren't rats," said
Susie. "Angelica was just
scaring you."

She gave them the gerbils
to hold.

"Gerbils are fuzzy," said Tommy. "They don't bite," added Chuckie. "And they don't growl," said Edwin. "But they *do* like to chew—on cardboard!"

Everyone took a turn at holding the gerbils.

"I need names for my gerbils," Susie told them. "Any ideas?"

"How about Frankenrat? Or Igor?" a voice said.

It was Angelica.

"You tricked me," she told Susie. "That was mean!"

"Well, you played a mean trick to keep the babies away!"

"Okay, okay," Edwin said. "Time to let bygones be bygones."

"Huh?" the babies said at once.

"Edwin's right," Susie said. She smiled and held out a gerbil. "Do you want to hold her?" she asked Angelica.

Angelica took the gerbil, which nuzzled her hand.

"Let's put them in their rockin' rollers," said Susie.

The babies chased the gerbils all over the floor.

Then they watched them chew pieces of cardboard into tiny bits.

"Hey, this one runs fast," said Tommy. "Can we call it Zoomer?"

"Sure, Tommy," Susie agreed. "And because this one tickles, I'll call it Tickles!"

"Zoomer and Tickles, the bestest gerbils in the world!" said Tommy.